A MAGIC CIRCLE BOOK

INSIDE THE RED AND WHITE TENT

written by **MARGARET MARY JENSEN**

illustrated by **GEORGE M. ULRICH**

THEODORE CLYMER
SENIOR AUTHOR, READING 360

GINN AND COMPANY
A XEROX EDUCATION COMPANY

3

Here is a tent,
  white and red.
Something inside
  is never fed.

A horse, a giraffe,
a lion too.
All in a tent.
Is it a zoo?

This is a lion.
    Here is his mane.
If he is a lion,
    what makes him tame?

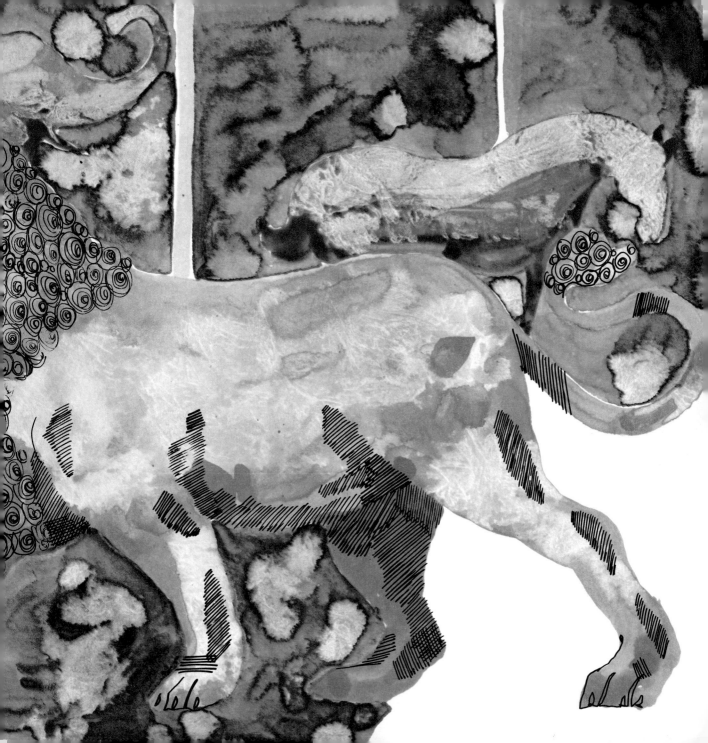

A pink giraffe
    I never did see.
If not a giraffe,
    what can it be?

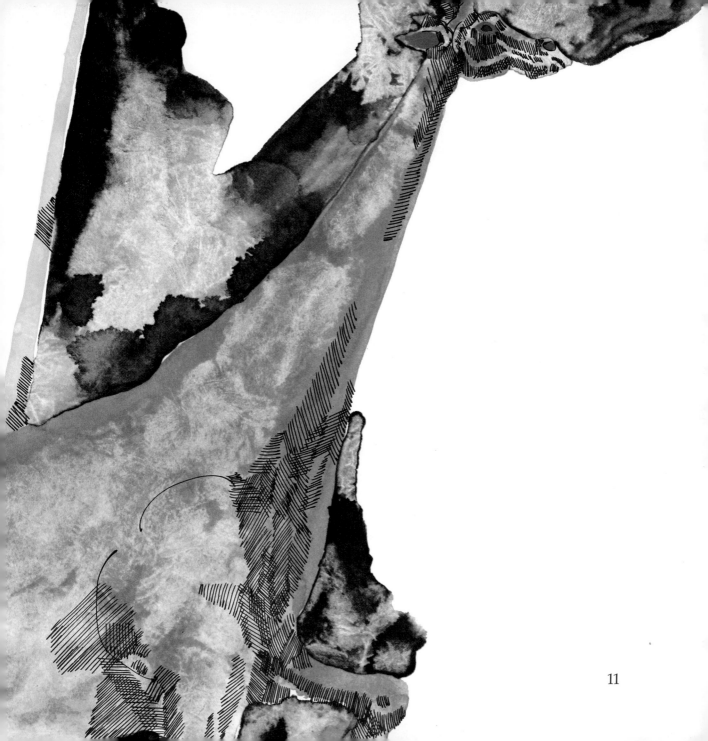

12

Is this a horse?
  It can't be.
Look at the legs—
  1, 2, 3.

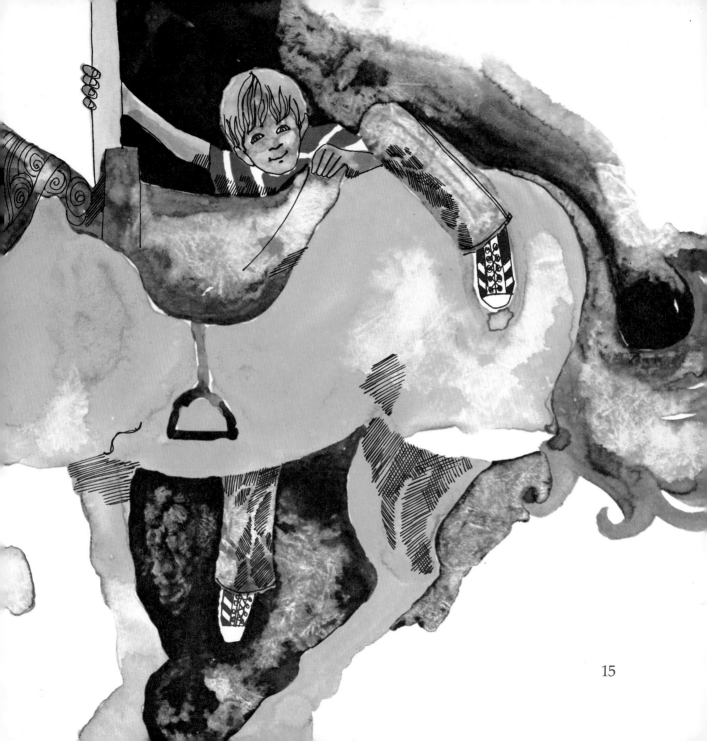

Who are you?
  Why are you here?
No one ever,
  ever comes near.

Do let me help.
  I can work for you.
I will make the animals
  look like new.

19

You are a big help.
But the work is done.
It is time to ride.
You choose the one.

HIJK **8**
Printed in the United States of America